The Animal Boogie

Debbie Harter

Barefoot Books
Celebrating Art and Story

Down in the jungle, come if you dare!
What can you see shaking here and there?
With a shaky shake here and a shaky shake there,
What's that creature shaking here and there?

IT'S A BEAR!
She goes shake, shake, boogie, woogie, oogie!
Shake, shake, boogie, woogie, oogie!
Shake, shake, boogie, woogie, oogie!
That's the way she's shaking here and there.

Down in the jungle where nobody sees,
What can you see swinging through the trees?
With a swingy swing here and a swingy swing there,
What's that creature swinging through the trees?

IT'S A MONKEY!
He goes swing, swing, boogie, woogie, oogie!
Swing, swing, boogie, woogie, oogie!
Swing, swing, boogie, woogie, oogie!
That's the way he's swinging through the trees.

Down in the jungle in the midday heat,
What can you see stomping its feet?
With a stompy stomp here and a stompy stomp there,
What's that creature stomping its feet?

IT'S AN ELEPHANT!
She goes stomp, stomp, boogie, woogie, oogie!
Stomp, stomp, boogie, woogie, oogie!
Stomp, stomp, boogie, woogie, oogie!
That's the way she's stomping her feet.

Down in the jungle where the trees grow high,
What can you see flying in the sky?
With a flappy flap here and a flappy flap there,
What's that creature flying in the sky?

IT'S A BIRD!
He goes flap, flap, boogie, woogie, oogie!
Flap, flap, boogie, woogie, oogie!
Flap, flap, boogie, woogie, oogie!
That's the way he's flying in the sky.

Down in the jungle where the leaves lie deep,
What can you see learning how to leap?
With a leapy leap here and a leapy leap there,
What's that creature learning how to leap?

IT'S A LEOPARD!
She goes leap, leap, boogie, woogie, oogie!
Leap, leap, boogie, woogie, oogie!
Leap, leap, boogie, woogie, oogie!
That's the way she's learning how to leap.

Down in the jungle where there's danger all around,
What can you see slithering on the ground?
With a slither slither here and a slither slither there,
What's that creature slithering on the ground?

IT'S A SNAKE!
He goes slither, slither, boogie, woogie, oogie!
Slither, slither, boogie, woogie, oogie!
Slither, slither, boogie, woogie, oogie!
That's the way he's slithering on the ground!

Down in the jungle where the stars are shining bright,
Who can you see swaying left and right?
With a sway sway here and a sway sway there,
Who is swaying left and swaying right?

WE ARE!
We go sway, sway, boogie, woogie, oogie!
Sway, sway, boogie, woogie, oogie!
Sway, sway, boogie, woogie, oogie!
That's the way we boogie through the night!

let's stomp!
(INDIAN ELEPHANT)

let's slither! (COBRA)

let's sway!
(PARROTS)

let's boogie!

(HORNBILL)

The Animal Boogie

Barefoot Books
Celebrating Art and Story

At Barefoot Books, we celebrate art and story that opens the hearts and minds of children
from all walks of life, inspiring them to read deeper, search further, and explore their own creative gifts.
Taking our inspiration from many different cultures, we focus on themes that encourage independence of spirit,
enthusiasm for learning, and sharing of the world's diversity. Interactive, playful and beautiful, our products
combine the best of the present with the best of the past to educate our children as the caretakers of tomorrow.

Live Barefoot!
Join us at www.barefootbooks.com

To Megs, Krissy, Erin and Jordie with wonderful memories of your singing and dancing at le Tupé
— love always, Mama
For Tuppence and Aeron — D. H.

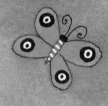

Barefoot Books
2067 Massachusetts Ave
Cambridge, MA 02140

Barefoot Books
124 Walcot Street
Bath, BA1 5BG

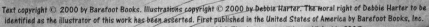

Text copyright © 2000 by Barefoot Books. Illustrations copyright © 2000 by Debbie Harter. The moral right of Debbie Harter to be
identified as the illustrator of this work has been asserted. First published in the United States of America by Barefoot Books, Inc.
and in Great Britain by Barefoot Books Ltd in 2000. This hardcover edition published in 2008.
All rights reserved. No part of this book may be reproduced in any form or by any means,
electronic or mechanical, including photocopying, recording or by any information storage and
retrieval system, without permission in writing from the publisher. This book was typeset in One Stroke Script Infant.
Printed and bound in China by Printplus Ltd. This book has been printed on 100% acid-free paper.

The Library of Congress cataloged the paperback edition as follows:
Harter, Debbie.
   The animal boogie / Debbie Harter.   p. cm.
   Summary: Rhyming text presents various animals as they dance their way in and around the jungle.
Includes music.
   ISBN 1-905236-22-0 (pbk. : alk. paper)
   1. Children's songs, English--Texts.   [1. Animals--Songs and music. 2. Jungles--Songs and music. 3.
Songs.]   I. Title. PZ8.3.H257Ani 2005 782.42'083--dc22 [E]2005013843

Hardcover with CD ISBN 978-1-84686-231-1
British Cataloguing-in-Publication Data: a catalogue record for this book
is available from the British Library

3 5 7 9 8 6 4

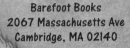